Cricket
Here & Now

SUDHIR TAILANG

ISBN 81-86685-46-4

Published by
Wisdom Tree
C-209/1, Mayapuri II,
New Delhi 110 064
Ph.: 28111720, 28114437

Cover Design: Kamal P. Jammual

Printed at
Print Perfect
New Delhi 110 064

From the Commentator's Box

This book is special for me. And I hope it's equally special for you too! I'm really delighted to present to you *Cricket Here & Now*. This is my first book based on the theme of cricket. I've followed cricket closely for years. In between, I lose interest in the game and totally ignore it! But the trouble with this game is that you can't!

Cricket is a religion in India. And like religion, it's a touchy subject too. It's tricky to make fun of it! A victory or a defeat is potential enough to incite a riot in India! But, nevertheless, it's a subject that offers immense possibilities and has always fascinated me.

In this anthology, I've tried to capture different aspects of the game of the willow! I've often used cricket as the sight-screen, and against this backdrop, I have bowled many political players out! The game provides a perfect pitch to depict political events on! I've drawn Vajpayee being attacked by the Opposition's fast bowlers! A match between Musharraf and Atalji! Shiv Sena, Bala *Saheb*, Togadia... internal politics of the parties-I've put them all in the cricket ground! After all, politics is a game, isn't it? And our leaders are playing games all the time!

The front-page pocket cartoon, Here & Now, does have enough of politics, but in this single-column box, I play with several other subjects as well. Cricket is a recurring theme in this space! From match-fixing to betting; from doping to modelling.... I've covered all the games that go on within and without the cricket ground!

In this collection, I've also added some fresh cartoons—specially done for this book.

Cricket has always excited me! As a young child I played cricket with the tennis ball in our *mohalla*. Then graduated to the cork ball, and finally to the red leather beauty!

I listened to the faint commentary on the radio when India played in West Indies or Australia or elsewhere. I recall those movies that I went to watch just to see the two-minute report of the test series with England in the Films Division Newsreel that used to be a fixture before the main feature. Today, in the age of live telecasts, it's impossible to imagine the mysterious pleasure that one got watching those two-minute clips in the movie hall!

Over the years cricket has metamorphosed into a totally different game altogether! The off-white ethereal innocence has been replaced by a ruthless multicolour multibillion industry! From a game it has transformed itself into an entertainment outfit-a sort of Bowliwood! But the magic of cricket has remained the same! I hope you will find some of it in these cartoons!

New Delhi **Sudhir Tailang**

Howzzat? I've got a stay order from the court! You're out and I'm in !

They've spoiled the whole pitch! Let's find out if they belong to the Shiv Sena !

He's the busiest lawyer in town!
The fellow specialises in cricket !

I am sure one of the Cola companies will hire him to endorse their cold-drink along with a cricket star!

*I've put all my money on Sachin —
let me find out how he is playing !*

The way our cricketers are playing,
I'm sure, they're drugged!

I know, Dad, 'Dazzler' is the national animal of South Africa!

With 5 kg of vegetables, you get this coupon! Ma'am, you can win a trip to South Africa!

Both India and Pakistan are pretty good at chasing each other's score!

No banned drugs, Doctor! I don't want to spoil his future as a cricketer!

He's a great cricket lover! He's throwing out all the products endorsed by our cricket stars!

Don't even touch it! It's something worse than pesticides! It's been endorsed by our cricket stars!

Yes, he's watching the match!
He's disappointed and angry with our team!

Only one of them can do brisk business at a time !

The latest score on the SMS, Swamiji !

We're an emotional people! He threw out these things endorsed by our cricket stars—only last week!

It's a cricket bat, Sir !!

What's the latest score, Saheb ?

Will they show the World War after the World Cup?

Sunday is a holiday for all of us—
there'll be no traffic at all!

They're watching live telecast of the War—from Johannesburg!

When you show a cricket match, it's called 'live' coverage ! But this is 'dead' telecast !

MLAs, MPs, ministers, judges, cricketers, bookies, bridegrooms. . . ! Soon we'll have no room for the ordinary criminals !

The boy is suffering from World Cup related stress ! Keep him away from TV

Who'd come to listen to us ?! They're all watching the World Cup !

We lost the match by two tickets—
they didn't let us in!

To promote the game of cricket, we're fielding 20 cricket stars in the Lok Sabha polls !

The score is : 2 for 5 ! 2 rupees in 5 hours !

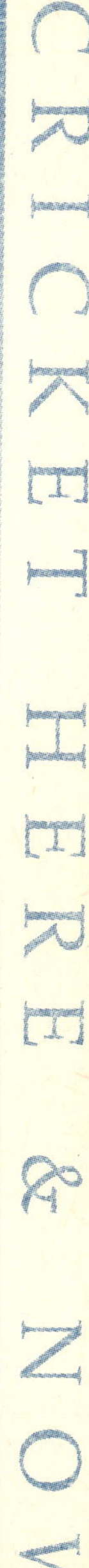

You know he uttered his first words today
— World Cup !!

He'll reshuffle the cabinet only after the World Cup Final !

He's brave too! Once, he had a fractured leg and sprained back-but he still rushed to the well of the House and walked out several times!

No, no, not a soap — he's watching a cricket match !

They've pasted a picture of the cricket ball and watching for the past two hours!

Cricket stars are cut out for Parliament ! Their experience of running between the wickets helps them in staging walk-outs!

She just switches off the TV ! She's pretty reformed now — Earlier she used to break TV sets if the Indian team lost !

If Sachin, Sehwag and Sourav play well — we'll win !

They do films, ads, TV shows—and all sort of things! I'm really surprised no cricketer has done a pop album!

He's watching old recordings of Abdul Qadir bowling !

That's Ganguly and Jayasuriya sharing the trophy!

Cricket is a game played with water bottles—not with a ball any more!

Babaji has announced his team for the 'Ramjanmabhumi Eleven' vs 'Babri Eleven' match !

The Bodyline series is Modi's favourite !

Must be the job of a cricket fan !!

One thing is clear—both the countries love playing games!

He's not an astrologer, but he can give you all the scores in advance ! He's a bookie !!

The pilot used to be a spinner earlier !

In this test, only South Africa are playing—the entire Indian team has been banned!

They're demanding reservation for lower castes and EBCs in the cricket team !

Of course it's an official Test match—between the BCCI, UCBSA and the ICC officials!

So, it's agreed then that we should include Paes, Bhupathi, Jaspal Raṇa and Vishwanathan Anand in our cricket team!

No advertiser wants me any more! Looks like I'll have to be content with just playing cricket for the rest of my life!

I can't make up my mind whether the cricket beat should go to our crime reporter or to the business correspondent !

Why are you wasting your time, Mom? Dad told me that the captain would score 17 before he's run out! And they'll be all out for 217!

Well, this is a one-stop sports shop!

Well, then, if Cronje is arrested-- you give me 15 lac! And if any of our cricketers is nabbed, I pay you 10!

Oh my God, we're yet to play the second innings !!

He says he wants to be a match-fixer when he grows up!

That's Mr Kumar's mobile. This one is Mr Chawla's picture...and over there you see a model of his London shop! And...

How did I get to know of it?
Well, Manoj told Sidhu, Sidhu told Mongia,
Mongia told Chandra,
Chandra told Vishwanath, Vishwanath told..

I'm told Prabhakar had enough tapes to run a 24-hour sports channel! So he's launched one!

For a bar of chocolate you threw the match?! Great! Some day you you'll lead the Indian team!

Unlike Cronje,
I don't have a spiritual advisor... but
I have a spiritual Bhai!

Is that a special scheme for cricketers only, Dad?

...and besides, these match-fixing allegations are a part of the conspiracy to destabilise the Rabri Government!

Let Joshi, Advani, Rabri Devi....
resign--then, I'll follow suit!

Perhaps he is the only cricketer in our country against whom there are no allegations!

Endorsements, logos, brand names.....this was bound to happen! He's investigating the match-fixing cases!

No, he's not a cricket star--he's a Samata Party MP!

I'm inculcating in him an interest in cricket right from the beginning!

There're three wickets in the game ! Nobody opposes that ! But they'll ban trishuls !

How was the MP's vs Indian Cricket Team one-dayer?

No, not with toys, he plays with mobile phones! I'm sure some day he'll become a big cricket star!

My husband is very upset about the Government's decision to call off the Pak cricket series! He is a bookie!

I'm told the BCCI is appointing another sleuth to assess the Madhavan report!

Let's announce our team,
and the schedule to disrupt the series!

Please believe me, Sir,
I'm not a Shiv Sainik.
I'm only a construction worker!

How about giving Duryodhana Awards to our cricketers?!

No, not the ad agency chap—it's a Bollywood director! He wants to sign you for a villain's role!

Hello, Police Station? Could you please provide security cover for my kids? They want to play cricket in the park outside!

PEACE
DOWN WITH BUSH
MAKE
NOT
WAR

ST BE
AN!
PEACE
NO WAR
DOWN WITH GANGULY

BE A SPORT-
DON'T SPOIL
THE GAME!
VHP

CRICKET

85

I.TAX

GUJARAT POLLS
CONG WIN PAK WIN

TWEEN 'INDIA' AND 'PAKISTAN'
MODI

NORMAL MONSOON
WASHED

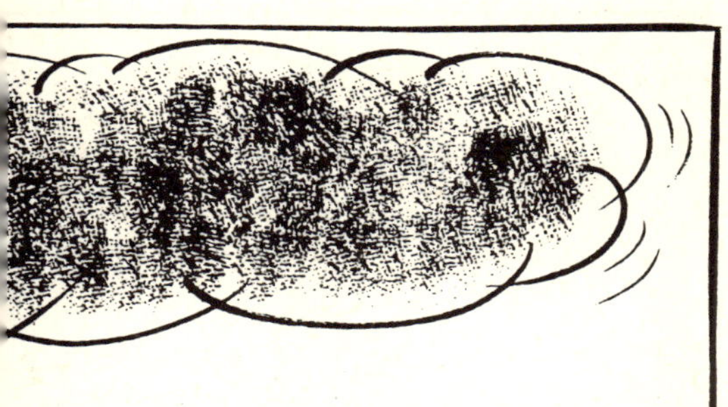

E THE GAME WILL BE
'S UNDER A CLOUD!

THE **CBI** IS NO MATC
FOR **HIS** PLAYING SKILLS

CBI

He's a special secretary to the selection committee! He's studying the horoscopes of our cricketers !

95

Let's build a cricket stadium in this area, sir !

All of them want to go to South Africa these days — to improve our ties with them !

No, we're not closed, but your work will be done only after the World Cup !

He loves cricket. He'll do anything to ensure India's victory! His vastu expert has advised him to sit this way if he wants India to win !

They're bringing a cricket star for campaiging ! I hope they also bring some cold-drink bottles that he endorses!

Honestly, I can't even spell cricket !
But I'm on all the important cricket bodies !